Fred Law Olmsted, Elisha Harris, J. M. Trowbridge, H. H. Richardson

Staten Island Improvement Commission a Letter Introductory

Anatiposi

Fred Law Olmsted, Elisha Harris, J. M. Trowbridge, H. H. Richardson

Staten Island Improvement Commission a Letter Introductory

Reprint of the original, first published in 1871.

1st Edition 2023 | ISBN: 978-3-38212-420-5

Anatiposi Verlag is an imprint of Outlook Verlagsgesellschaft mbH.

Verlag (Publisher): Outlook Verlag GmbH, Zeilweg 44, 60439 Frankfurt, Deutschland
Vertretungsberechtigt (Authorized to represent): E. Roepke, Zeilweg 44, 60439 Frankfurt, Deutschland
Druck (Print): Books on Demand GmbH, In de Tarpen 42, 22848 Norderstedt, Deutschland

Staten Island Improvement Commission.

A

LETTER INTRODUCTORY

FROM

MESSRS. OLMSTED HARRIS TROWBRIDGE AND RICHARDSON.

1871.

EDGEWATER, Dec. 22d, 1870.

To the Staten Island Improvement Commission:

GENTLEMEN.---Before completing the work which you have given us to do, we wish to obtain the results of an analysis of waters from several sources on the Island, and certain other promised information, and our report will thus be delayed until your next regular meeting.

We have thought it might be well for us, however, to define in advance, our views of the general line of policy to be adopted in a comprehensive scheme of improvements for Staten Island, thus explaining, to a certain extent,.the grounds upon which our final propositions must be recommended to your approval, and this will be the object of our present communication.

We wish to so far forecast the future market of this metropolis for real estate, that we can be satisfied what of its demands Staten Island in particular may be prepared to supply with the greatest certainty of large, general, ultimate profit.

All possible demands of the future may, in the first place, be broadly divided under the heads of Commercial and Domestic; domestic being understood in this case to refer not only to dwellings but to whatever would administer directly to household economy, convenience and comfort, including stores, shops and markets, for local supply.

The eastern margin of the Island, from a little north of Tompkins landing nearly to the Yacht Club House, has advantages of a peculiar character for certain commercial purposes, deep water and good holding ground being found close off shore, and large shipping being less liable to be troubled by ice than at any other point in the harbor at which it can lie with equal safety and convenience in other respects. An extensive use of these advantages would lead to the building of a special class of warehouses, factories and shops along the shore. As, within narrow limits, this demand is liable to become an imperative one, the erection of many permanent and costly domestic buildings on this shore is not to be expected. The sooner, therefore, its commercial advantages are developed the better.

Beyond this district, we do not think that a commercial demand for real estate is ever likely to be of much importance, or that it should be courted, for the Island, and as we are advised that a different opinion is held by some of your Commission, we wish to explain why.

In any region where the value of land depends chiefly on its agricultural productiveness, as, a generation since was the case here, any undertakings that are calculated to improve its means of communication with a distant market, or to establish a market within it, can hardly fail to benefit the landowners, who, consequently, are often asked to aid in the introduction of them. Nearly all of the territory of the United States being in that condition, there is naturally a pretty strong public opinion about the interest and duty of landowners in this respect. But Staten Island is now very differently situated from the country in general. It has no difficulty in finding a market for its crops, or in finding shipping enough to move them. What advantages, then, can it expect to gain by courting commerce?

In answer we may be pointed to the value which real estate has acquired in the commercial quarter of New York Island. Staten Island has a much greater extent of shore on the same harbor than New York Island, and while it is considerably nearer the sea, it is also approachable to better advantage from the main land, especially by railways. Does it then seem unreasonable to expect that by adding certain artificial to its natural advantages, so much of the commerce of New York can be drawn to Staten Island, as will greatly advance the value of its real estate?

The question is how much—how many acres—of the whole area of the island is likely ever to be actually occupied, do what you will, for commercial purposes? We think we can show that it is very little indeed.

If we look at the two parts of New York city as divided, say, at Fourteenth street, we shall see that one side is mainly occupied for commercial purposes the other for domestic. Imagine, then, that this division had been made more perfect, and that it had not been confined to the politically limited New York city, but had included all of that larger New York, now numbering a population of nearly a million outside the city, which sends a deputation of men every day to its commercial quarter. Under this division it will be evident that the buildings of the domestic class not only already cover a great deal more ground, but that *their number and area of occupation is enlarging much more rapidly* than that of the commercial class, and this notwithstanding, perhaps. that the amount of business transacted, of goods exchanged, is larger than ever before.

It is not very difficult to see some reasons why this should be so, and why it is likely to continue.

In the progress of commerce, men of marked ability have more and more duties pressed upon them, and duties in undertakings of the most diverse character. The necessity of personal conference in regard to affairs requiring separate offices, gives increasing value to time during certain hours, and distance is for these purposes yet equivalent in the market to time. Hence vicinity to various offices becomes an increasing element of value.

The increasing specialization in business which often makes many sources of supply necessary to be called on for a purpose which could formerly be served by one, tends in the same general direction; the result being always an increasing motive to compactness.

At every center of commerce, consequently, more and more business tends to come under each roof, and, in the progress of building, walls are carried higher and higher, and deeper and deeper, so that now "vertical railways" are coming in vogue.

It may be thought that these observations apply only to commerce in a restricted sense, that is to say to exchanges and administration, and especially not to manufactures and shipping. The question is important because some think that it may be possible to establish a great manufacturing quarter of the metropolis on the island, and with this in view a different line of policy might be advised from that which we shall assume to be required. It is well known that conditions which make a difference of many years in the expectations of life with operatives are no obstacle of consequence to the success of manufactories. Let us then examine the facts.

There are between four and five thousand manufacturing establishments on New York Island, with an aggregate capital of about $70,000,000. Why are they on New York Island rather than anywhere else?

Not because of cheap land. cheap building materials, cheap food and lodging for operatives; not because of cheap coal, or wood, or water-power, or taxes or insurances. For all manufacturing purposes in which these conditions are of primary importance, building sites must be sought far away, not only from New York but from Staten Island.

It is true that for certain of the latter class of purposes cheapness of transportation to and from the island of New York becomes also important. But the cost of transportation lies chiefly in the loading and unloading. Distance, within certain limits, extending far beyond Staten Island, counts but little. Moreover such disadvantages as distance establishes are lessened by every extention or improvement or addition to the roads, boats, telegraphs and mail facilities which connect the outer country with the town. They will be less in the future than they are at present. Thus the difficulty of establishing new centers or new sub-centers of manufacturing, like Newark, has, of late years, greatly increased and will continue to increase.

Dividing then, all manufacturing purposes for which land and buildings are liable to be required, into two classes, one of which economy will place at a comparatively remote distance, we see that, with respect to the other class, the same motives operate as with reference to buildings simply for the exchange and administrative offices of commerce—motives, namely, which favor a tendency to increasing compactness of association; to higher and deeper buildings, and to the occupation of less and less land relatively to the whole amount of the trade of the port.

The increasing use of large, deep, fast steamers, lying but a few days at the wharf, and each carrying in a year to and from any given hundred yards of shore ten times the burden of the old fashioned coasting craft, and the increasing employment of steam and machinery in handling and stowing cargoes, tends to make dock room of less and less value relatively to the whole amount of freighting business to be done at the port. General McClellan's plans will aid this tendency.

The length of shore front on navigable water within ten miles of the City Hall is about eighty miles, of which a tenth part only, and that all more than seven miles away, is on Staten Island; of the seventy miles perhaps twenty is now in constant demand for the accommodation of shipping; of the remaining fifty an important part, as yet unavailable for shipping, will soon be improved by undertakings in which the cities of New York and Brooklyn and leading railway corporations are now engaged. The land lying immediately back from the shore, to the extent of several thousand acres, is flat and easily adapted to manufacturing and other ordinary commercial purposes. It is on the other hand generally unattractive, and cannot easily be made, even tolerably, suitable for domestic purposes. We submit that at any rate of progress which past experience gives us reason to anticipate, and especially in view of the shrinking tendency in respect to ground-space which we have shown to exist, it will be a great many years before any considerable part of the land thus available and thus likely to be pressed on the market, will be required to be occupied by buildings, docks, or other structures for commercial purposes.

If not, then it is certainly impracticable, by any use of the taxable and other political resources of the county, to place Staten Island so successfully in competition for supplying the limited amount of land that is going to be wanted in the extention of the commerce of the port that any important favorable general effect upon the value of its real estate can be expected to be produced.

On the other hand, it is only necessary to go out on Long Island a little north and east from Brooklyn to see how harmful an effect is liable to result from a very moderate effort in that direction, many people of wealth who formerly lived there, having been driven away, and tracts of land formerly clothed with beauty laid waste almost as by an invading army, this being the result of a number of scattered manufactories. It is true that there are manufactures which would not be likely to have any such effect, but it is also true that manufacturing establishments started for one object are liable, after a time, to be adapted to another, and that those which have the greatest permanency in the outskirts of large towns are such as are most offensive, and destructive of value to the better class of domestic property near them. Illustrations of this are not wanting on Staten Island. It is also to be considered that it is very difficult to draw the line between a manufactory which is legally permissable, and one which is legally a nuisance, and that when capital has been once largely invested in any works, it is always a difficult and expensive undertaking for the public to remove or control them. The owners of property in the district we have referred to on Long Island, having first invited the introduction of manufactories, have of late years made great but vain exertions to cause the removal or suppression of many of them.

Turning now to the domestic division, is there, in the first place, any question that a tendency prevails precisely opposite to that which we have seen to be governing the commercial—a dispersing and colonizing tendency? If it is recollected that the people who inhabit the tenement-house districts of New York are very little to be taken into account, simply because they are just those who are least able to get what they want, and consequently manifest least what is generally wanted, for domestic purposes, we think there can be none.

A man who has probably made more money by suburban real estate improvements than any one else in the country, said to us lately, " I find that everywhere there has been the largest advance where the streets have been widest and the lots deepest, and if, where the determination of the width of streets and the depth and breadth of lots has been under my control during the last thirty years, I had, in every case, insisted on having them doubled, I should have been at least a million dollars the better for it. I will never again, if I can help it, have a street laid through or beside property of mine in the outer part of a town, less than a hundred feet wide, nor lay off lots less than fifty feet wide and a hundred and fifty feet deep, unless it is where I wish to draw commercial business or a poor class of people for a special purpose, as where hands are needed for a factory."

Is this experience and opinion exceptional? If so, why, over so large an extent of ground on New York Island, in Westchester and in Kings and Queens has the plan upon which land was laid out twenty thirty and forty years ago been discarded?

This plan was generally that of rectangular blocks of 25x100 feet lots, with streets of from fifty to seventy feet in width, a plan tolerably well adapted to purely commercial requirements. The new plans are less regular and will give larger blocks, wider streets, deeper lots and more open spaces. This, according to our reading of it, is simply an adjustment of the market to a rising demand of a special character for domestic purposes, which can be met on New York Island only by a compromise with the commercial demand, and consequently, at the best, but imperfectly, but which, with the small exception we have referred to, the whole of Staten Island may be adapted to supply in the most complete way and with great and speedy profit to its land-owners.

From an examination of the recent census returns, which we have been permitted to make at the Marshall's office, it is ascertained that in one district, over twenty square miles in extent, about as far north from Wall street as the middle of Staten Island, there has been an increase of population during five years of over ninety-five per cent.; in another sixteen miles distant, a little larger, forty-four per cent.; in another twenty-five miles distant, or further than the most distant point of Staten Island, fifty-five per cent. These are all in Westchester County; and, from personal examination, we know that the larger part of the immigration has consisted of thrifty families, each carrying with it considerable capital, and almost invariably going into villas and cottages, with more or less extensive grounds.

There are a number of districts on Long Island and New Jersey where an increase of a similar character has occurred quite as large.*

* The increase in population on Staten Island in five years has been less than sixteen per cent. The average capital per head brought in and made available for taxation has been less than it has in some of the districts above referred to, which have increased much more rapidly. There are several districts in Westchester and Long Island, as near and as accessible as the most favored of these, which, as we perceive by the census returns, have either lost or failed to increase at all in population, and the real estate of which is believed to have fallen in value. We have either visited or had communication with physicians and intelligent citizens in each of these, and, in every case, the first reason given for the depression of their real estate is a reputation for unhealthfulness.

The suburban travel (chiefly commutation), on five railways from which we have returns, has, during the last ten years, more than doubled the number of passengers increasing from four to nine millions: on other routes the rate of increase is believed to have been still greater. On several of the suburban boat lines the travel has more than doubled in four years.

The out of town families, some member or members of each of which habitually visit the island of New York daily, now number fully three quarters of a million, and within two years will exceed the resident population of the city. What part of this number is strictly suburban, that is to say, resident in detached dwellings with sylvan surroundings yet supplied with a considerable share of urban convenience, it is not possible to ascertain, but it is certain that the proportion of this class is very rapidly enlarging.

Land held in farms fifteen to twenty years ago, since broken up into plots of from one to five acres, in the midst of attractive scenery, having a fair general reputation for healthfulness, approached by tolerable roads, and accessible in from half an hour to an hour from Wall Street, has almost invariably advanced in value at least five hundred per cent, and often a thousand.*

The tendency, thus indicated, is not peculiar to New York; it now prevails in every other large town, in London and Paris, as well as in Boston, Philadelphia, and in our Western cities. Everywhere townspeople have been lately tending to break town bounds. It may, to be sure, be regarded as a mere fashion, which, acting first on the richer and more luxurious classes, and sending them for the summer only to country seats, then taken up in a little different form by a large number of people of more moderate wealth, has at length fairly laid hold of the masses, in which case it must be expected to soon run out, and be followed by a reaction. But if it is a mere fashion, and has this liability, it is at least singular that it should for years, while sufficiently manifest, have been less powerful, and made its way more slowly at the Head Quarters of Fashion than generally elsewhere.

Regarding it not as a fashion but as a sensible and permanent common movement, the reason why it has been more subdued at Paris is not difficult to see. Obviously it is because at Paris the old theory of a town has been till now essentially maintained, which made it a fortress, enclosed it by walls, and necessarily surrounded the walls by a waste of land, in which domestic considerations were required to yield to military.

If we look closely at any large city, it is to be observed that this

---

* This statement is made on the authority of Mr. Homer Morgan.

outward current is by no means setting all in one direction, nor does it benefit all points alike in any direction. Some districts are constantly avoided or fallen upon only by the thriftless, and for evident considerations of necessity rather than choice; others are passed clean over, so that sometimes land at a distance is more in demand than that lying between it and the point of departure. We shall hold not only that the general flow, but that all these leapings and turnings of the stream, wherever it has any strength and persistency, are the result of perfectly comprehensible laws, the working of which has been manifest in other forms for centuries. To agree on what class of improvements Staten Island requires in order to derive from it the greatest benefit, there must first be a common understanding of these laws. To carry out such agreement there must be a common faith in them, and in what they will, if heeded, ultimately accomplish. We shall briefly indicate, therefore, the general line of evidence which leads to the convictions in this respect which will govern our recommendations.

A century ago much of the filth which at present is taken off by sewers in most of our large towns was thrown out into the street, under the windows, in front even of the most noble mansions of the richest of cities, and often remained there for months polluting the air, and unquestionably greatly shortening the average period of life of their inmates. Less than a hundred years earlier, the dining rooms of the best houses in the healthiest city of England were at frequent intervals laid over with a wash of soot and small beer to hide the dirt which was allowed to remain upon them. Still another hundred years back we find the dining rooms of rich men's mansions strewed with rushes in order to absorb and partly cover the still greater amount of filth which was customarily permitted to accumulate on them, table-forks having then been but recently introduced, and such offal as bones, cartillage and apple-cores being often dropped from the fingers upon the floor.

We find from evidence, the character of which these facts illustrate that there is a fixed tendency among civilized men, to place more and more value upon the cleanliness and purity of the condition of theirs domestic life, and a little consideration will show that this law is not confined in its operation to the interior of dwellings, but extends to all that may surround or be associated with them.

Now it is impossible to have a high degree of cleanliness without great inconvenience and cost in connection with many conditions of commerce. Much that would be offensive in and about a dwelling house must be endured in and about a factory, a wharf, or even an office frequented by men engaged in many of the duties of commerce.

Hence, in looking even but a little way back, we see how rapidly, since town walls have become generally less important, the tendency has been developed to separate domestic from commercial life. Late in the last century the largest bankers and merchants of London, Amsterdam and Paris, still maintained their domestic and commercial establishments under the same roof, and the Stewarts and Tiffanies of the day had a door opening between their show rooms and their family dining-rooms.

The constantly increasing distinctness of separation between the commercial division, and the compact domestic division, in all large modern towns, is one result of this law of progress; another is the gutters, gratings, sewers and water-works by which a large share of the filth which was formerly endured in and about the house is rapidly taken to a distance, and which have made it possible even to move about within the town without coming in direct contact with anything very obviously dirty. These improvements have been so great, and their results so beneficial, that the average length of life of the classes of the people who live the year through in the city of London has been doubled. But it has not yet been found practicable to keep the air of compactly-built parts of towns pure and sweet, and lives are yet shortened and made painful by the privation. It is doubtful if it will ever be possible to overcome the difficulty of doing so in localities of a certain density of population where the two great natural agents of disinfection, sunshine and foliage, cannot act largely and freely throughout the streets, and on each side of every house. In fact, beyond a certain point, density of residence is incompatible with a high degree of cleanliness or a high degree of health, comfort and civilization. The difficulty is vastly increased if to the thronging of mankind is added the liability of dust, dirt and unwholesome emanations of various manufactories.† Here then is one reason why our great cities will never be able to retain within narrow limits the families of those who are engaged in their exchanges and manufactures. They will be able to do so less and less. By modifying their plans, making larger blocks, wider streets and more numerous and broader public places and parks, they may bring the necessary evils of compact building within certain bounds, but the process must go much further than it has yet done, even in Paris, where, in fifteen years, $375,000,000 was spent in this

† In nearly all large commercial towns in Europe great undertakings have been planned, and in some carried out, for securing more space in and about the dwellings of that part of their population which, by its avocations and its poverty, is practically precluded from moving into suburbs. Liverpool has recently expended over $5,000,000, and Glasgow has just made a loan of $16,000,000, payable in twenty years, for this purpose.

way, or in London where $24,000,000 has just been spent on sewers alone, before the migration to a considerable distance from the commercial districts, of the classes most advanced in civilization, will cease to grow constantly larger.

———

There is one other motive element in this movement to which it is necessary to allude—the esthetic. There is no doubt that with the advance of civilization there is in the mental constitution of civilized men an increasing susceptibility to certain forms of beauty, especially to the beauty of nature, apart—so far as it is possible to regard it as ever apart—from associations of health and comfort. In what degree this element guides the suburban movement it is hard to say, but that it is of some consequence and increasing consequence, is proved by the extent to which it is abused in the course of catch-penny speculations. Nothing has been more common of late than to recommend building sites on account of the natural beauty of distant prospect which they possess, or the local attractiveness of the land itself which is offered for sale, when the process of building and of so called improvements in the neighborhood will assuredly destroy both. It may seem hardly necessary to say that views of woods which will soon be felled, streams which will be turned into sewers, meadows that will be built on, landscapes that may be shut off, are of no permanent value in a home, but it is certain that they are accepted as such in thousands of cases, and that they enter largely into the fictitious valuation of real estate which causes so much distrust and confusion in regard to permanent conditions of value.

There are few things which make greatly for the happiness of men concerning which they know so little of the process by which the happiness comes, and the conditions on which it depends, as this of the beauty of nature. It is the commonest experience that men destroy beauty under an idea that they are going to increase it.

But most men will, at first sight, prefer a coarse colored lithograph which is dear at a dollar to a Claude or a Murillo, which has, nevertheless, during hundreds of years been regarded as a treasure, and for which there are to-day not a few men who would gladly give many thousands of dollars. And it is prob- able that there are not a great many who, having the painting placed where they would see it, without any effort to force admiration, several times a day for some years, would not learn also to place something like the true market value upon it. Undoubtedly it is the same with the beauty of natural landscape, and the beauty of parks and gardens. Men do not know on what their enjoyment of one locality more than another depends, but they find that one permanently contents them more than another. And upon the degree of general contentment which can be assured to any community, will the value of the real estate of that community in the long run wholly depend.

———

In dealing with a question like this, of the most economical means of *permanent* improvement for a large area near a great center of business, nothing is more important than a realization of the utter folly of a policy which has heretofore been often followed with profit by individual speculators in a small way. To illustrate the danger of it we shall refer directly to local experiences.

Within the memory of several of your members, and since the childhood of most, the value of nearly all the land on Staten Island was established by reference solely to its advantages for fishing and agriculture. One-third of the appraisement of what were then the most valuable farms was due to the fishing rights which were sold with them. The demand for dwelling-sites by men engaged in business in New York began between 1830 and 1840. The probability of its increasing soon occurred to many persons, and upon this farms began to be bought and held idle " on speculation," along the East and North shore.

We propose to briefly and, of course, imperfectly, trace the history of a single district of from a thousand to fifteen hundred acres in extent, which, in the judgment of many, was at that time the most attractive of any on the island, or even perhaps of any on this side of the Atlantic. The land had been held for generations by the descendants of the original settlers. Their interests being divided between fishing and agriculture, but little of the ground was kept under the plough, most of it was in wood or broad greenswards. Old trees had an unusual value, ship builders from New York being wont to run down the bay, and select timber for special purposes in the woods, buying it standing. Hickories of a certain size and form were also in request for the fisheries. The woods were thus managed in a way not very common with farmers, a certain class of trees only being picked out and felled for ordinary purposes, and those promising special profit allowed to remain and spread broadly ; the groves were therefore notable for their beauty, and something of this may be seen in portions of them yet remaining.

The owners of the land lived in quaint and cozy, low-roofed and broad-galleried cottages, approached by the most delightful class of summer roads, winding among the great trees, crossing clear brooks and skirting the smooth clean meadows. A man might search the world to find an alternative to the commercial town more complete or more pleasing. It was believed also by the best physicians of New York to be a place of distinguished healthfulness, and there is yet no reason to doubt that it was so. The apparent objections to it were merely the difficulties of access, the badness of the roads in the Winter and Spring, and the want of society.

The land traders, when their time came, promised to remedy these objections; a wharf was to be built, and direct steam communication established with New York, roads were to be constructed and each of the farms was to be divided into a number of places adapted to country-seats and villa sites, inviting to a good class of residents. This was chiefly undertaken by an association and so far as it was able to obtain possession of land it at once laid out a broad straight highway through it, crossing the shallow valleys upon low causeways. A wharf was also subsequently built, and direct steamboat communication for a short time maintained with the city. No substantial improvements in the way of drainage were made, however, nor was the slightest thought given, apparently, to securing to the public in the future any claim upon the preservation of the various elements of health and beauty which now gave the land really the better part of its value.

The expectations of profit of those who engaged in these enterprises were to a considerable extent realized. Numerous places were sold, houses built and grounds laid out. To the original reputation of the district for the beauty of its landscapes and its detailed and local rural charms was added a renown for the attractions of its villas, gardens and society. All choice sites rapidly advanced several fold in value.

Another class of changes began to be noticeable between 1845 and 1855. Such improvements as we have described had drawn not only a considerable number of families of great and moderate wealth, but also many with little or no accumulated means, who were employed as laborers and servants. The steam ferry made the island generally known to holiday excursionists. A lager beer garden was established to aid the ferry enterprise. The ground least saleable for villa residences began to be occupied by shops and small dwellings, stables and vegetable gardens, to make room for which fine trees were often felled. Several of the original suburban places became nearly enclosed by those of the later formation, and thus less valuable for their original purpose.

At length two or three factories were established in the neighborhood, increasing the demand for small lots for lodging houses, stores, and dram shops, thus still further lessening the attractiveness and the value of a certain part of the territory for suburban purposes. The means of livelihood of some of the later arrivals being precarious, when hard pressed they helped themselves to fuel, which they found first in the old farm rail fences, and then in the unenclosed woods which remained. Large tracts of these, consequently, were cleared soon afterwards by their owners. The construction of roads across the valleys had in several cases arrested the natural flow of water upon the surface, and some of the old water courses not only lost all their beauty, but, from the mingling of household wastes with the water made stagnant by obstructions, became disgusting and dangerous. Some places presently began to be known as unnealthy. All soon came under suspicion.

An intelligent stranger could now no longer possibly reach the parts which retained any of the original conditions of attraction, to look at a site offered him for a residence, without having the question raised :

"Suppose I come here, what grounds of confidence can I have that I shall not by-and-by find a dram-shop on my right, or a beer-garden on my left, or a factory chimney or warehouse cutting off this view of the water? Is this charming road sure not to be turned also into a common town street, strewn with garbage, and in place of these lovely woods, can I be certain that here also there will not soon be a field of stumps with shanties and goats and heaps of cinders? If so what is likely to be the future average value of land in this vicinity? Whatever advantages it still possesses over other districts about New York as a or rural or suburban dwelling-place, it never can possess any for compact building at all superior to a hundred thousand acres elsewhere about the city. Looking either with reference to enjoyment of it as a place of residence, or as an investment for my children, I must be cautious not to be too much affected by superficial appearances. *What improvements have you here that tend to insure permanent healthfulness and permanent rural beautifulness?*"

We know that in certain cases, this course of reflection and inquiry has operated to prevent the sale of places, and we also know that since the conditions to which we have referred have been very distinctly manifest, the rent and market value of a large number has declined or at least ceased to advance, while at the same time, the number of people going out of town in search of places of residence has vastly increased.

There is another district on the island which, within twenty years, has been made accessible from the city in half the time that it was previously, taking contingencies into account and with reference to practical connection with the commercial center. It was believed, and confidently predicted by able business men that the completion of the railway, by which, mainly, this has been accomplished, would double its real-estate value. We find that, in fact, it is doubtful whether the gold value of land in this district has advanced at all. We know of several cases in which land has been recently bought at a price considerably less than that at which it was sold fifteen or twenty years ago.

Surely, it will be said, this is a very extraordinary case—a suburban district of great beauty, declining in value of real estate apparently because of being brought nearer to town, and this, at a period when in other directions suburban real-estate has been advancing five and ten fold in value! But it is not at all extraordinary that a suburban district loses attractiveness when the interests of its landowners are turned from agriculture to idle speculations. In this case obstructions to drainage have been permitted to occur and accumulate, common highways have been neglected, and hundreds of acres of beautiful woodland have been cut away, leaving bare, unsightly wastes in their place to mortify the eye, and making pestiferous swamps of low lands, the superabundant moisture of which was formerly sucked up and harmlessly evaporated by the foliage. The district is much less healthy, and the pleasure with which a family, having any feeling for natural beauty, can reside in it is not nearly as great as it was twenty years ago. Consequently it is less adapted to the market, and, of course, is all the time tending to fall, instead of rising in value.

We could easily enforce our argument by reference to several localities in various parts of the island, giving, if it were proper to do so, names and figures. We could point to one short piece of road laid out and "improved" in the usual way of land traders, in the midst of a district which had previously been flourishing, and by which a series of attractive, small villa sites was opened up and placed in the market. The local outlook was interesting. A pretty stream which ran near by skirted by a nice grove, was regarded as an advantage, as properly managed it certainly would have been. Access to broad distant land and water views was direct, short and convenient. More than twenty houses have been built on this road, the grove being cut away to make room for them. As population has come in malaria and other sanitary evils have been developed. The original builders have nearly all sold out and moved away. A real estate agent having charge of some of the houses tells us that for several years past there has been increasing difficulty in finding good tenants for them and rents have been largely reduced. The physicians inform us that this year, not one household upon this road has escaped a visit from diseases which are caused by poisoned air. In the densest wards of New York or London, there has been no larger per centage of preventable disease, and in none have diseases been found to fix themselves more firmly upon the system, and to offer stronger resistance to remedies.

Looking to see what had been the more indirect effect in the neighborhood we ascertained that a house which, during a long series of years, had been a favorite summer boarding-house—frequently rejecting for want of room more applicants than it was able to accommodate had this year not been half filled. A large villa was pointed out to us, standing on an eminence overlooking the row of houses we have spoken of. It had been sold by its original owner fifteen years ago at a certain price, since considerably improved, sold again last spring at one half the same price, had been unoccupied during the Summer except by a man hired to live in it, and is now offered at a reduction from the price paid for it last Spring.

We do not wish that our remarks should imply censure. However desirable and profitable it may be, where capital can be commanded, there is no obligation upon the owners of land to prepare it suitably for the residence of a community before putting it in the market, and very few, any where, are ever found disposed to do so. As long as the houses in any district stand well apart, with an abundance of trees about them, and only the more healthy situations are occupied, the dangers which threaten a closer neighborhood do not generally very distinctly appear. They may at least be guarded against by individual care. If, however, easy access from the city and low prices for land tempt immigration, with denser population the healthfulness of any locality is liable to become questionable; once established, from year to year the doubt increases; with its increase the prospect of any considerable future advance in the value of land diminishes. The owners at one time elated, become discouraged; they distrust the market value of radical improvements, and are more than ever unwilling to undertake them privately. At length, before they know it, a state of things is reached in which it becomes questionable whether any general combination, supposing it could be brought about, to secure them would effect a sufficient change in the reputation of the neighborhood to make it profitable.

It may be best to inquire here how far this doubt applies at this moment to Staten Island as a whole.

There are parts of the Island which now suffer from an undeserved reputation for unhealthfulness. There are various localities, further from the city, less attractive in landscape, and less healthy, which stand much higher in the real estate market. There are other places upon the Island, the reputation of which is locally worse, but concerning which we are obliged to say, after examining the physicians who practice in them, and after personal inquiries from house to house, that the worst has not been told. But whatever the shortcoming of public rumor toward them in particular, it is more than made up by the reputation which is fastening upon the Island in general. This growing bad reputation, damaging to the value of every acre upon it, we have found to be greater at a distance, and among people who had never seen it, than anywhere else. It is surprising how far it has already gone. It has been manifested in the most exagerated form by new-comers from Europe and California. We have more than once seen it expressed in letters of travelers published in distant parts of the country.

Such a one in passing the healthiest part of the Island, including a locality of considerable breadth in which we find no evidence that a single case of malarial disease of local origin has ever been known, is led to exclaim, "What a Paradise!" whereupon his companions are represented as saying "Yes, if you don't find a Paradise on Staten Island it will not be because fever and ague will not do its best to help you," and the writer adds "It is quite true that this Island is as unhealthy as it is beautiful."

How is this to be arrested? How can it be prevented from going on from bad to worse? Never by voluntary individual exertions, never by local action, never by proceedings of one or two of the towns, for as long as a single locality remains in a state to justify it, it is impossible to prevent the undeserved reputation from being applied to the Island as a whole by the general public. And *if* it goes on, according to all experience, the consequences may, at no distant day, be absolutely disastrous. Nothing is more sorry than the fate of any district, which, lying near a great town, gets a bad character strongly fastened upon it. Capital avoids it in all forms except those in which its coming is resisted by all localities in which the hope of better things has not been abandoned. There is unquestionably a tendency to let things drift in this direction among some of the land-owners on Staten Island.

We may as well here as any where, perhaps, state our conviction that some of the local undertakings now in progress, which are expected to relieve real estate from the bad name which has been found to be growing upon it, are liable to result in still further disappointment, not only for the reason which has been given—namely the impossibility of inducing the general public, from which any considerable improvement of demand must come, to discriminate between good and bad localities upon the island—but also on account of the superficial character of these works, and the great expense and difficulty which will be found, if any attempt is made, to keep them in efficacious condition. This is so marked in some cases, that we are satisfied that the evil sought to be removed, will, in fact, be aggravated by them.

But let us ask what are the grounds of hope that Staten Island shall yet make head against this danger?

Harlem, ten years ago, had a place in public esteem much lower than Staten Island has yet reached. Its malarious condition was a constant subject of newspaper banter. Since then a very extensive and costly system of drainage has been carried out, and there is no more joking about Harlem flats. The old reputation seems already quite forgotten; and recent sales are reported at eight thousand dollars a lot for land which, ten years ago, before drainage and street improvements, was held and was unsaleable at five hundred.

The report, of your Committee on Organization, incidentally states that at New Brighton the value of real estate is higher, and has advanced more steadily during a series of years than at any other point on the Island. What is the reason of it? A large part of New Brighton is a remarkably well drained, and in all respects healthy district. It not only commands a magnificent view, but owing to the slope of the surface, it has been impossible to wholly cut off that view from any point. No part of it is compactly built upon. The houses are generally unobtrusive and inoffensive, wholly untownlike, and are surrounded by grounds with a variety of flourishing trees. Its roads are lighted, its wheelways macadamized, its gutters paved, its walks flagged and their slopes and borders neatly sodded.

If the reason is not to be found chiefly in these circumstances we think it will be difficult to account for the low market value of some other land which we have seen—land which, with good roads, could be reached as soon from New York as that midway between Brighton and Tompkins landing; land which is equally elevated, which commands equally fine distant views, which with drainage would be equally healthy, but in the foreground of which there is a pond hole and a raw bank and a gully, which fronts on a road of steep grade, always toilsome to climb and in the Spring liable to be almost impassable, and which is without gutters or side-walks or gas. Land of this description can be bought at a quarter of the price asked for that with which we compare it at Brighton.

The hope of Staten Island lies in the certain large profits of the substantial improvement of its low-priced lands.

But we have been met by men of large experience with the remark: "Staten Island is on the wrong side of the town. Fashion always goes one way and in New York it sets to the North, just as in London it sets to the West."

It is perfectly true that the Eastern outskirts of London are inhabited almost solely by very poor people, that the town extends in that direction very slowly, and that the progress of building in the finer class of residences has constantly been to the Westward, but why? If fashion, what established the fashion? Simply the fact that the town began to grow on account of its commerce, that it stood at the head of ship navigation on the river, that East of the uppermost anchorage, the banks of the river were low and flat and the outlook dreary, while to the West the ground was high and dry, and there were most attractive landscapes.

So far as town houses are concerned the drift of fashion to the Westward has thus been simply a matter of necessity; beyond that there is no drift to the Westward. Ten miles out of town to the Eastward there is as much of fashion and wealth as there is at the same distance in the opposite direction. The villas are as numerous and as fine. The noble seats of Sir Culling Eardly Eardley, Lord Say and Seal, and the Duchess of Sutherland are examples of them—and there are thousands of fine places in the same general direction nearer than that to the town. Whoever has looked upon the country which was near to the South and East, from the terrace of the Crystal Palace at Sydenham, before the view of it was lost behind the host of suburban houses that have been lately built in that direction, will remember that here is a fine elevated, healthy, well-wooded district and that it is studded with villas, country seats and parks.

It is the same at Paris—the best quarter of the town is in the North, in the South are factories and factory people. But go *ten miles* to the Southward and you find the banks of the Marne entirely occupied by villas and suburban villages, to which the Parisians who have no country seats resort for furnished apartments during the Summer. It is a beautifully wooded, healthy, and most attractive suburban district and fashion has nothing to say against it.

Is it fashion that prevents people from selecting Staten Island as a residence? We have known three cases this year in which families of wealth and high social standing, have, after looking at Staten Island, gone past it and found residences to the southward in Monmouth County, New Jersey. One of these had just abandoned a fine place at

Newport, on account of the inconvenience of going there and returning. They went to a place south of and much more inconvenient than Staten Island, simply because of the advice of their physician, that it was more healthy.

We have, during this inquiry for your Commission, visited several of the more successful suburbs—suburbs in which real estate has advanced, and is advancing very much more rapidly than at any point on Staten Island. At none of these are there natural conditions as valuable, in some respects, as at various points on Staten Island; but on the whole we find reason to believe that the chances of securing health and happiness to a family in the long run are but little overrated in the market value of land.

We say but little, because there seems to be some reason to suspect that the long course of make-shifts to which the public has been subected by men "making haste to be rich" on small capital, has at last had the natural effect of giving excessive market value to land, where the artificial requirements of a good suburban neighborhood are well provided for in a permanent way.

Evidence of this is not limited to the vicinity of New York Bay. Let us look to a point where sheer speculation has run wilder, and paper streets and paper towns have, for a time, been worth more than probably anywhere else for an equal period in the world. Recently two suburban speculations were started near Chicago, one at a distance of six, the other of nine miles from the town, each centering upon a station of the same railway, on land worth, at the time, from one to two hundred dollars an acre. The managers of one laid out their plan in the usual way, made streets of the prairie soil, with neat open ditches, and spaces for side-walks beside them; planted trees, hit upon a good name, got up their lithographs and advertised. The managers of the other borrowed a large sum of money at a high rate of interest, mortgaging not only the land they were to operate on, but other property for the purpose. With this they first underlaid their land with several miles of draining-pipe, then built macadamized roads with paved gutters, iron gratings, concrete side walks, and broad borders, frequently spreading into little greens and commons, planted picturesquely. All the natural wood and the banks of the stream which passed the place, were made public property, and shelters, seats, bathing and boat houses were provided upon it. An Artesian well was sunk, and with a steam-pump water sent to all parts of the property.

Before these improvements were nearly complete the owners began selling land upon the roads at twenty dollars, and soon afterwards advanced their price to thirty dollars, the front foot. The place has just been lighted with gas, the works being an independent undertaking, and no land can be bought at present on the improved roads at less than forty dollars. It is not two years since the work was begun. Over forty private houses have been already built upon the sites sold, a number of them at a contract price of over twenty thousand dollars. The engineer in charge of the works writes us, as to the effect on the neighborhood, that one tract, which is partially inclosed by the improved territory, and barely touches at a corner upon one of the macadamized roads, and which was valued two years ago at from $80 to $100, has been recently sold at $1,000, an acre. All surrounding property has advanced 200 per cent. during the last year. With regard to the enterprise nearer town, it is a complete failure, it stands to-day as it did a year ago, not the first house having been built upon it.

We turn from this lesson in the West to another of equal significance which comes to us from the opposite quarter. East of the City of London, there are districts to which we have already referred, in which, among dust-heaps, brick and coal yards, and large waste places, there are clusters of habitations which from their wretchedness have been spoken of in Parliament as a national disgrace. Efforts have sometimes been made to relieve the dampness, which is the primary cause of the abandonment of these districts by every thing which is wholesome and decent; but, until recently, they had always been of a superficial penny-wise, pound-foolish character, resulting in disappointment. One such was alluded to by Mr. Dickens, in a description from which we draw, with slight contraction of the original, the following account:

"In such a neighborhood stands Jacob's Island, surrounded by a muddy ditch, known in these days as "Folly Ditch." A stranger looking from one of the wooden bridges thrown across it will see crazy wooden galleries common to the backs of half a dozen houses with holes from which to look upon the slime beneath; windows broken and patched; rooms so small, so filthy, so confined, that the air would seem too tainted even for the dirt and squalor which they shelter; wooden chambers thrusting themselves out above the mud, and threatening to fall into it—as some have done; dirt-besmeared walls and decaying foundations, every repulsive lineament of poverty, every loathsome indication of filth, rot and garbage; all these ornament the banks of ' Folly Ditch.' "

Six years ago it was determined by the authorities that one of the worst of these wretched eastern parishes should be, as far as the streets and public property were concerned, thoroughly improved. Matters were so bad that plans had previously been discussed for a whole-sale deportation of the inhabitants. What actually was done included the construction of a sufficient number of deep under-ground drains, falling into a main, which extended to a distance, the road-ways were macadamized, and tar concrete walks laid by the side of them, water was laid on, and gas lights provided for. To accomplish this, it was necessary to raise money by loans, payable in fifteen to twenty years. Mr. Fisher, the engineer, employed to superintend these improvements, is now in this country. He informs us that before they were well completed, the old shanties and pestilent-rookeries began to be laid low through the voluntary action of the owners of the land, and that in place of them, now, less than six years from the outset of the work, may be seen hundreds of attractive cottages and villas, with neat grounds about them. A healthy and thriving popula-tion, able to bear a large taxation has come in, and although no exact statistics can at this moment be furnished us, there is no doubt of a great profit from the undertaking.

In the extended observation of the different members of our Board on both continents, not an instance is known in which similar results have failed to follow works of improvement judiciously adapted to provide good roads and walks, and well drained and healthful building sites, with attractive sylvan surroundings within convenient distance of any large town.

The effect of substantial suburban improvements, even where un-necessary for health, is not at all mysterious. The outgoing townspeo-ple do not reduce their standard of comfort in any respect materially, and they soon become discontented if they go where the degree of study and forethought, and skill in management of household affairs which they are accustomed to use is very greatly augmented. People moving from the country to the town rapidly lay aside habits of careful pro-vision in respect to many details of housekeeping. They keep but small supplies, and wait till they are nearly out before taking thought for their replenishment. It is nothing to call or send to the grocer's or the butcher's or the baker's, when anything which they supply is found to be wanted. But the distance of a quarter of a mile over a bad country road is a much greater difficulty to a housekeeper than three or four miles upon a clean firm flagged street. A well fifty feet deep comes as a severe blow often repeated. Kerosene lamps all over the house and utter darkness outside the door give constant anxiety. Considerations of health being equal, it is the degree in which objec-tions of this class to a residence prevail, here and there, that chiefly determine the direction of the suburban currents.

There is no doubt of an increasing domestic demand for land divided on a larger scale than has hitherto been generally adopted, or than is desirable, where commercial convenience is the primary consideration. A question remains as to the extent of the enlargement demanded?

Of this, the course of reasoning we have followed enables us, perhaps, to form some idea. Houses, for instance, must be so far apart, that the air of each shall be absolutely free from contamination arising from any other or from the highways; the highways must be so far apart, so spacious, so furnished or flanked with trees that organic waste can not be carried from them, to an injurious extent, into the houses between them; that the air passing across them shall be quickly disinfected or screened of whatever it takes up that is filthy. If a highway is short—taking little or no through traffic, requiring a wheel way of not more than 22 feet, the mininum thus reached would but little exceed the space of the ordinary town arrangements, except in the size of lots.

What then, is required to be possessed by each family, for its private use, out of doors, beyond what can commonly be had within towns?

We answer that a high state of health, or a sound moral condition can never be acquired by children or preserved by adults under the requirements of success which modern town life tends to impose, where it can not be made easy and convenient to spend considerable time out of walls—more time than can honestly be spent in idleness or in occupations which, with us, are deemed consistent with publicity. For this purpose there needs to be attached to every house a series of out-of-door apartments, not open to public view, in which direct exposure to sun and wind may, when desired, be avoided, and in which various ordinary household occupations may be carried on. One of these should connect with the kitchen, another with the social rooms of the family; there should be turf on which young children can walk, and fall without injury, on which girls can romp without soiling their dresses; there should be a dry walk for damp weather, a sheltered walk for windy weather, and a sheltered sitting place for conversation, needle work, reading, teaching, and meditation.

We repeat, that with the exciting and engrossing interests of the stage of society which we are now reaching, arrangements such as these are essential to a high state of health in a family. Every physician will endorse this statement. We can dispense with them as our ancestors could dispense with chimneys and table forks, with cotton and silks, with potatoes, sugar, coffee and tea; but it will cost us more to dispense with them than to obtain them, and learn to use them. Sooner or later all civilized people will learn to use them.

These requirements involve no large amount of land; but the minimum can not be much less than twice that of our present ordinary town lot.

How much must be added to this in order to admit of any degree of artistic luxury and completeness will depend very much on situation. With good, shaded highways, walks not liable to be overthronged, it is not at all necessary that the house should command fine distant or general views, it is rather better that stand-points for these should be possessed by each family in common with others, at some little distance from the house, so as to afford inducement and occasion for going more out from it, and for realizing and keeping up acquaintances by the eye at least, with the community. To give children a fair chance to develop their individual tastes and talents, however, without disturbance to neighbors, even with the most wholesome family discipline, the space of private ground must be enlarged, under most circumstances, to at least what would be inclosed in a parrallelogram of fifty by one hundred and fifty feet. Where less than this is taken it will soon be from necessities of poverty, not choice.

It is not desirable that the lot should be a parallelogram or of any regular and uniform shape, on the contrary, it will be more satisfactory if it is not. It is much easier to fit a house and grounds agreeably upon a space of land, the sides of which are not parallel and the angles equal than upon one of the ordinary town-lot form.

Can we get any idea of the maximum? Suppose that two, three, or four hundred thousand families are to be in competition for land, each needing to have one member, at least, spend the larger part of each day in close proximity to the center of business; obviously the maximum for each will eventually be fixed chiefly by considerations of the cost of the land, established by competition, within certain limits of distance; and the limits of distance as far as time of passage is concerned will be, up to a certain point, constantly enlarging in every direction.

Yet we do not think that the progress of invention is to tell so much in the improvement of the speed with which distances can be overcome as in the cheapness, frequency, regularity and *comfort* of transportation. The question will be between cost of passage and cost of land; the nearer, other things being equal, the more valuable the land and the less of it must be accepted for what each man can afford to pay. But the measure of cost for passage will not be wholly in the value of time required for it and the fare; the incidental occupation of the time will be an important item. At present there is scarcely a suburb of New York the time to reach which from Wall Street, is not, on an average, worse than lost, that is to say, so far from being passed profitably, it is passed most expensively—at great cost of nervous energy, health and comfort. An addition of ten per cent. to the cost of running the Staten Island ferry boats, with good roads and walks from the landings, would make it possible for most men to be in the way of gaining health, of receiving enjoyment, of spending their time profitably, doing two-thirds of all that would be given to the necessity of passing from Wall Street to their home.* Nothing like this can, as yet, be asserted of any other line of exit from the town, and there is no reason to suppose that any form of land communication will ever be invented by which, without vastly larger cost, it will be possible to make the time occupied as valuable as it may be now made in water conveyance.

The greatest improvement will probably occur, however upon common highways. which there is no difficulty in carrying to the point at which one horse can do the work which must be given to three on our present roads. It is not improbable, also, that steam omnibuses will soon come into use, and that these, running from landings and stations, at a speed of ten or twelve miles an hour, will call at all houses on the highroads, whenever required, as the old coaches did. There are, at this moment, no practical difficulties in the way of this method, except those with which any new arrangement of general public utility has to contend. There are already in different parts of the world over four hundred steam carriages working successfully on common roads. But better and generally wider roads are the first requirement.

When there shall be, as there soon will, two or three hundred thousand families to be provided with houses out of town, the least space wanted by each of which shall be what we have named—and when the possibility shall be realized of occupying the best part of an hour's time of transit not uncomfortably, competition will then fix such a price upon all land within an hour's distance of the city, that only men of exceptional wealth, and tastes for rural domestic life, will think it best to pay for the use of more than eight or ten times as much of it as the amount we have named as the minimum for health. The ordinary size of the house lot which will soon be most in demand in the suburbs may thus be approximately estimated. Along the shores, where sites can be reached by a short walk from the steamboat landings, it will probably be from quarter to half an acre. Wherever there is a tendency to reduce it much below this, men will prefer to spend more

* The boats have most uncomfortable seats, are badly ventilated, and at night badly lighted. Being, also, short-handed, or with inadequate organization of service for their duty, passengers suffer from disorder and nuisances which might easily be prevented. These little matters make all the difference between misery and comfort to many, especially many women.

time on the passage, go farther and enjoy the use of more space. At a distance from boat landings, a larger area will be generally wanted to compensate for the greater trouble of land conveyance, and men who can afford to keep horses will also be able to afford to buy more land. Sites then will be in demand large enough to admit of some luxury of personal property in local landscape. The maximum, under ordinary circumstances, within an hour of Wall Street, on elevated land, and in a healthy and well furnished neighborhood, is not. in our judgment, likely to permanently exceed five acres. The average for all the more attractive parts of Staten Island, clear to its furthest extremity, beyond distances within an easy walk from the shore, would be less than that, but certainly not less than one acre. If the interior land should be cut up in smaller plots than an acre, most people will prefer to pass a little more time on the public conveyances, and go further. This is to be inferred from the readiness with which thousands are now induced to travel by the most fatiguing and expensive means of conveyance to much greater distances than Tottenville, to gain no advantage except that of controlling a little more land for their money.

If our reasoning has been good, we have thus determined with some approach to definiteness for what form of real estate there is likely to be in the early future the largest demand in the vicinity of New York. To what extent that demand shall go, and how rapidly it shall be developed is a question in all probability of the completeness and rapidity with which a supply shall be provided for it to be fed upon. In any locality where such building sites have been provided as we have described, from a quarter of an acre to five acres in extent, well drained and in all respects healthy; approached quickly, cheaply, and with any tolerable degree of comfort from New York; where good service of tradesmen and public servants may be had, where water and gas may be laid on, where pleasant natural scenery is accessible, and where these characteristics extend over a sufficient breadth of country to give assurance of a suburban domestic neighborhood of a permanent character—in any locality which comes near offering these advantages —the indications of experience all are that if twenty thousand building sites could be put in the market, there would be twenty thousand families glad to buy them at once, at prices a good deal more than double the present average value of all the land on Staten Island—and it is hardly to be doubted that if they did so, there would be one hundred thousand people healthier, happier, richer and better for the bargains. We do not know where one such site can be had near New York to-day at ten times the average value of land on Staten Island.

The result of our study thus far has been to suggest a doubt whether there is any safe intermediate ground between an abandonment of the Island to the condition of an outskirt quarter of the metropolis, which, while it may increase in number of population, will lose in quality—an outskirt which will tend constantly to compare less and less favorably with the more fortunate suburbs—and an undertaking of improvement which will be likely to give it the first rank among them for healthfulness and general convenience, and which will have the result we have described, of causing twenty thousand detached villas and cottages, to be soon built upon it by capital to be brought from without and thus made available for local taxation.

We will go further and say that we have been led far toward the conviction that the position of the Island with reference to the center of business, and its natural attractions, are such, that if it could be relieved of its bad reputation in one single particular, the public would accept temporary inconvenience in other respects, taking the risk of delay in improvement of access, of roads, of water supply, and of other common suburban requirements, and that the Island, relieved from the single disadvantage to which we refer, would rapidly advance to the position of the best suburb, and its real estate command the highest rates of the market.

The one particular to which we refer is of course its unhealthfulness, and its special unhealthfulness depends simply and solely upon malaria. Aside from malaria troubles it has always been the healthiest suburb of New York.

The problem of malaria will be considered in a second letter. Without present argument upon the latter point, therefore, the views of general policy which we now desire to commend to you may be briefly re-stated as follows:

The value placed by the more far-sighted, prudent and prosperous part of the public, first on healthfulness, second on convenience, third on beauty, especially on rural beauty, in choosing their residence is constantly and rapidly increasing. This increase does not depend on fashion but on fixed laws of civilized progress, it is then likely to continue and may be depended upon as permanent.

The territory conveniently accessible from New York which has any prospect of retaining an agreeable rural character, and which is now free from malaria is limited. The rural territory which is likely soon to be retrieved from malaria is still more limited.

If Staten Island can be freed from malaria, it will be a comparatively easy matter to make it the healthiest, and at the same time the most convenient and most beautiful suburb of New York.

As soon as this character can be established for it a practically un-limited demand for its real estate will occur—a demand which will rapidly multiply the value of every acre of land upon it.

Respectfully,

FRED. LAW OLMSTED,
ELISHA HARRIS,
J. M. TROWBRIDGE,
H. H. RICHARDSON.